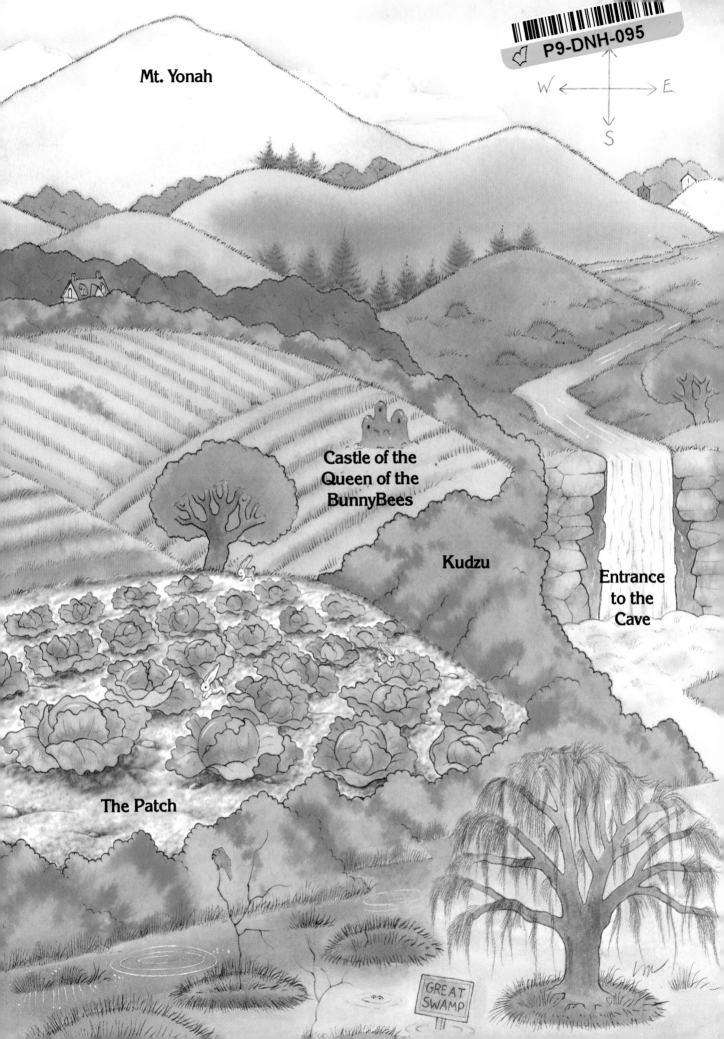

To Kathy—
The winner in
reading and reporting
on the most books.
Mrs. Kelly
6/20/85

Kara
Seidler

Library of Congress Cataloging in Publication Data: Taylor, Mark. The shyest kid in the patch. (Cabbage Patch kids). SUMMARY: When Sally Faye is born in the cabbage patch, she is very shy until her new friends are threatened by a mean jackrabbit.
[1. Friendship—Fiction]   I. Lace, Lynn, ill.   II. Title.   III. Series.
PZ7.T2172Sh   1984   [E]   83-26262   ISBN 0-910313-30-X
Manufactured in the United States of America   1 2 3 4 5 6 7 8 9 0

The Shyest 'Kid
in the 'Patch

Story by Mark Taylor
Pictures by Lynn Lace

Now, you all know that each one of the Cabbage Patch
Kids is different. Some like singing. Some like sports. And
some like nothing more than sitting a spell and dreaming.

Some of the 'Kids are noisy. Some of them are quiet. Some of them are friendly as frisky pups. And then there are others, who are shy.

This story is about one of them.

Ever since Sally Faye had been born, she had been shy. She was so shy that when the other 'Kids went on a picnic, she stayed home and read.

When the other 'Kids picked sides to play a game, she stood on the outside of the group, and then drifted away to pick flowers all by herself before anyone got a chance to pick her for a team.

She started off toward **Blue Hole** where she knew
Sally Faye sometimes went to be alone, but instead of
finding Sally Faye, she met Marilyn Suzanne and went over
to tell her of her plan.

Otis Lee shrugged his shoulders, and gave Cap'n,
who was one mighty worried-looking dog, a pat to let
him know that it wasn't really his fault. Then the two of them
went back to join some of the other 'Kids in a game of tag.

Now Gilda Sue had seen what had happened with Otis Lee, and she thought to herself, "I know Sally Faye wanted to make friends with Otis Lee, but she's just like a minnow, the least little ripple sends her scurrying off.

She's too shy to let herself have fun." Then and there Gilda Sue made a vow to make friends with Sally Faye and help her get over being so shy.

Otis Lee once tried to be extra special nice to her.
"Hey, there, Sally Faye," he said as he walked up to her.
"Hey, Otis Lee," said Sally Faye quietly as she
looked down and rubbed the toe of her shoe in the dust.

"Look who I brought to see you," said Otis Lee, "My bulldog, Cap'n. Would you like to pet him?"

Now Cap'n was a friendly dog, and when Otis Lee introduced him to Sally Faye, he wanted to show her that he liked her, so he jumped up. When he jumped up, sad to say, he knocked Sally Faye down.

"Oh, help!" cried Sally Faye. She scrambled to her feet and quickly ran away.

"Sally Faye, Wait! He didn't mean to . . ." yelled Otis Lee, but it was too late. Sally Faye ran to the other side of the Cabbage Patch . . .

. . . and she never looked back.

The following day Gilda Sue left a special bunch of cookies for Sally Faye to find.

And on the day after that when she found Sally Faye sitting all alone, she said, "Sally Faye, I have a brand new skipping rope. Would you like to skip rope with me?"

Sally Faye smiled shyly and nodded her head. Before very long, Gilda Sue had a shadow, and that shadow's name was Sally Faye. Everywhere that Gilda Sue went, Sally Faye was sure to follow.

"I am glad that Sally Faye finally has a friend,"
said Cousin Cannon Lee to Ramie as they were fishing,
"but she still doesn't seem very friendly. Do you think she likes
any of the rest of us?"

"I don't know," Ramie answered. "It's hard to tell. Gilda Sue
says she does, and I guess we'll have to take her word for it."

Gilda Sue spent a lot of time with Sally Faye. She found out that she had been right – Sally Faye was a wonderful friend. However, Sally Faye was still afraid to make friends with the other 'Kids, and Gilda Sue was beginning to think that her plan to get the 'Kids to know Sally Faye had failed.

Then one day, all by herself, Sally Faye showed all the Cabbage Patch Kids just how special she was. Here is how it happened.

Many of the 'Kids had gone out into the woods to pick blackberries. The blackberries were particularly plump and juicy that season, and all the 'Kids, including Gilda Sue and Sally Faye were so busy collecting berries that they didn't realize that danger was lurking nearby.

As Gilda Sue reached out to pick a particularly big berry, she heard a horrible snarl. She looked up and there, scrambling through the underbrush, was a huge, mean-looking jackrabbit.

It was Cabbage Jack! "Come here you nasty 'Kid," snarled Cabbage Jack. "I've got better work for you than this in Lavendar McDade's gold mine."

Terrified, Gilda Sue began to run. "Come on, Sally Faye. Run!"
All the 'Kids ran, but Cabbage Jack got closer and closer.

He reached out, grabbed Gilda Sue and began pushing her into a sack.

When Sally Faye first saw what had happened to Gilda Sue, she started running faster in order to get away from the terrifying jackrabbit, but then she slowed down.

Finally she stopped and turned.

Cabbage Jack was so surprised to hear such a big voice coming from such a small 'Kid that for a few seconds it was as if he had turned to stone. Sally Faye took advantage of his momentary shock, put her hands on her hips and glared at Cabbage Jack. "Why you mean, moth-eaten, no-account rabbit. You let that girl go. Gilda Sue is the first friend I ever had in my life. I like her, and I'm not going to let any oversized bully of a rabbit take her away."

And with that Sally Faye ran up and gave the jackrabbit a kick in the shins. "Take that, you ugly thing!" she yelled.

Cabbage Jack let out a mighty yell and reached down to grab his throbbing shin. As he did, he eased his grip on the bag, and Gilda Sue, who had been kicking and pushing from inside, forced her way out, grabbed Sally Faye's hand, and together they and the other 'Kids dashed back toward the Cabbage Patch.

Cabbage Jack, still holding his shin with one scraggly paw, tossed the bag into the blackberry thicket in disgust. "Lavendar's going to skin me for this!" he muttered to himself as he limped back to his mossy den.

When the 'Kids got back to the Cabbage Patch,
Gilda Sue caught her breath and told everyone how Sally Faye
had saved her. "She was really brave," Gilda Sue said,
"and she wasn't scared of Cabbage Jack one bit."

Sally Faye just looked down and blushed.

"Why, you're not so shy after all — at least when it counts." said Cousin Cannon Lee.

"That's right," said Gilda Sue. "There's really no such thing as being shy if you think of other people instead of yourself."

Now to be sure, it took a while for Sally Faye to get over her shyness; things like that don't happen overnight, even in the Cabbage Patch. But the more she worked at it the easier it got, and it wasn't too long before she was playing tag, joining in sing-a-longs and sharing secrets with her new friends.

Gilda Sue was happy to see the change in Sally Faye, so she was very surprised to find her all alone down by Blue Hole one day.

"Sally Faye!" Gilda Sue exclaimed. "What are you doing here all by yourself? I thought you'd gotten over that."

"Oh, I still like to be by myself sometimes." Sally Faye explained. "But now when I'm alone, it's because I want to be, not because I'm hiding."

Gilda Sue understood what Sally Faye meant, and she smiled to see her new friend so at ease and happy. Then she sat down next to Sally Faye and the two friends talked and talked until the sun began to set over the Cabbage Patch.

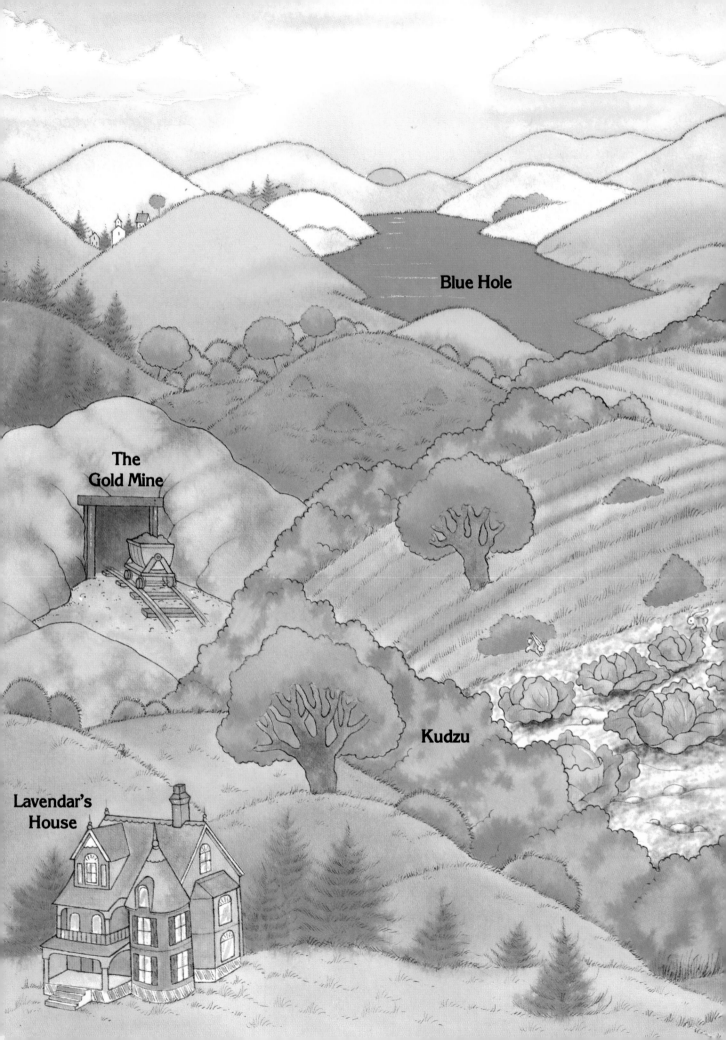

Blue Hole

The Gold Mine

Kudzu

Lavendar's House